The Animal Train
and Other Stories

The Animal Train
and Other Stories — by

CATHERINE WOOLLEY

Illustrated by ROBB BEEBE

WILLIAM MORROW & COMPANY
New York 1953

Grateful acknowledgment is made to the publishers of the following magazines for permission to reprint stories first published in their pages:

Humpty Dumpty, for "The Animal Train," "Mrs. Hen's Vacation," "Johnnycake for Ronnie," and "The Shiny Red Rubber Boots"
Child Life, for "A Sandwich for Smoky"
American Junior Red Cross News, for "Whistley Jim and the Wrong Side of the Bed," "Where Is the Carrousel?" and "The Cat That Wanted To Be Useful"
Topix, for "Dawdling Douglas"

With love to Susan
who always wants
"One more and that's all!"

Contents

The Animal Train

One windy, wintry day a baby bunny came hopping out of the woods. He hopped to the railroad tracks. The baby bunny looked down the long shining rails. He thought, I'm a big brave explorer. I'm going to find out where the tracks go. He hop-hopped along to see where the tracks went.

The baby bunny met a big rabbit. He said,

"I'm a big brave explorer. I'm going to find out where the tracks go."

The big rabbit said, "Silly! Why don't you hop on a train and find out where the tracks go?"

"Good idea," said the baby bunny.

He waited till a train came along. It whizzed by so close it almost whisked off his whiskers. The baby bunny was disappointed.

He hop-hopped along till he met another big rabbit. He said, "I'm a big brave explorer. I'm

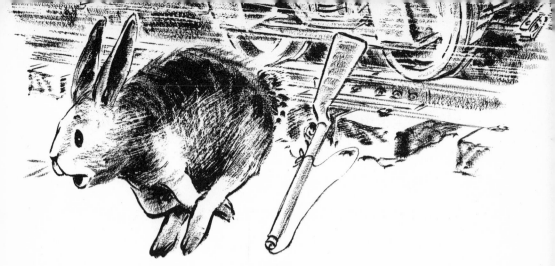

going to see where the tracks go. I tried to hop
on a train, but it whizzed by so close it almost
whisked off my whiskers."

The big rabbit said, "Silly! Trains only stop at
stations."

"Oh," said the baby bunny.

"And by the way," said the rabbit, "rabbits
can't ride on any old train. You will have to wait
for the animal train."

"Oh, thank you," said the baby bunny.

He hopped to the station. He hopped up to the
station man. He said, "I'm a big brave explorer.

I'm going to hop on the animal train and find out where the tracks go. When does the animal train come?"

"The what train?" said the station man.

"The animal train," said the baby bunny.

The station man thought. Then he said, "Sure enough, there *is* an animal train. But it won't be here for ages. Would you care to wait?"

"Well, all right," said the baby bunny. "Don't forget I'm a big brave explorer, though."

"Oh, sure," said the station man.

The station man began to build a little house out of a box. He made a warm bed of thick straw in the little house. He fastened wire netting across one side to let in light and air. He made a little door. He turned the little house with its back to the wintry wind.

"Who's that for?" said the baby bunny.

"Oh, nobody," said the station man.

The baby bunny was getting sleepy. He said, "I might as well wait in there." He went into the little house and curled up in the thick straw. He felt warm and safe. He could see the tracks. He liked the little house. He went to sleep. When he woke up, he said, "Will the animal train come soon?"

The station man said, "Oh, I guess so. Have a carrot?" He held out a crisp, plump, juicy carrot toward the baby bunny.

The baby bunny loved carrots more than anything. He sat in his snug little house and ate the carrot. It was delicious. Then he looked out at the tracks. He thought, Soon the animal train will come. I will hop on. I will find out where the tracks go. He thought, I can't *wait* till that animal train comes!

He said to the station man, "You didn't forget I'm a big brave explorer, did you?"

"Of course you're a big brave explorer," the station man said. "Have another carrot." The baby bunny ate another carrot.

One day the station man said, "The animal train is coming."

The baby bunny's whiskers quivered with excitement. He hopped out of his little house. There was a great chug-chugging. The animal train thundered into the station. The baby bunny's eyes popped out.

It was a circus animal train! In one car rode giraffes with necks as tall as trees. In the next car rode lions and tigers and bears in cages. In the next car were monkeys climbing and swinging about. In the next car were great huge elephants with long trunks.

The baby bunny said in a small voice, "Are they going to the place where the tracks go?"

"Yes, they are," said the station man.

The baby bunny thought very fast. He said, "I guess I'll take the next animal train." He scurried back into the little house. The animal train with all the dangerous animals aboard thundered on.

The station man said, "I'm glad you're going to stay for a while."

The baby bunny, safe in his little house, said, "But I'm still a big brave explorer."

The station man said, "Sure. You can take the next animal train. Have a carrot?"

The baby bunny nibbled the carrot. "I *might* not take *that* train, either," said the baby bunny. And he went to sleep in the thick warm straw.

Whistley Jim

Whistley Jim was a whistle on top of a factory. The factory was in a little town called Cloverdale. Whistley Jim was the only factory whistle in Cloverdale. "There goes Whistley Jim," the people said, when they heard him blow.

He was very proud of his town.

His tall smokestack looked down on the neat stores on Rolling Stone Road, with their awnings to keep out the sun. He could see Henderson's meat-and-grocery store, Coogan's drugstore, Tony the barber's, and Phil the vegetable man's.

He could see Crabapple Street with its white houses and flower gardens filled with petunias. He could see the village green where the band in their neat uniforms played music on summer evenings. He could see the brick school where the children learned arithmetic and history and how to spell *Mississippi*. He could see the red firehouse where the shiny red fire engine lived.

He could see his own factory. The factory was

neat, with green vines growing on it and green grass around it.

Almost all the fathers in Cloverdale, except Mr. Henderson the meat-and-grocery man, Mr. Coogan the drugstore man, Tony the barber, and Phil the vegetable man, worked in Whistley Jim's factory.

Whistley Jim was proud of helping to run the town. Every morning at seven o'clock he gave a soft, pleasant *toot* that said, "Time to get up, everyone!"

Then all the fathers got up and shaved. All the mothers got up and fixed the cereal for breakfast. All the children got up and tied their own shoe-laces.

Pretty soon Whistley Jim gave a loud whistle that said, "Time to go to work, everyone!"

Then all the fathers took their lunch boxes

(with sandwiches and bananas in them), and waved good-by, and started for the factory. All the children kissed their mothers and hurried off to school.

After that, Whistley Jim rested until time for the twelve o'clock whistle. That was a good whistle! Sometimes he whistled a couple of minutes early, just for fun.

"Time for lunch, everyone," the whistle said.

There was one more whistle—the five o'clock one. Whistley Jim liked that one best. He had a special tune for five o'clock:

      whoo   whoooooooooooooooooooo.
    whoo whoo   whoo
    whoo   whoo   whoo
    whoo   whoo whoo
  Whoo   whoo

And *that* meant, "Time to go home, every-one!"

When they heard the five o'clock whistle, all the fathers stopped working, put on their coats, and hurried home (not forgetting their empty lunch boxes, of course). All the mothers put on the kettle for supper. All the children put away their bicycles and went in to study their lessons. And when everyone was safely home, Whistley Jim's work was done.

One morning Whistley Jim needed oiling or something, so he woke up feeling cranky. "What can I do that's *bad?*" said Whistley Jim. "I know," he said. "The baddest thing I can do is to blow very early, *long* before seven o'clock. I'll make the people get up when they're feeling so-o-o sleepy! That will be fun!"

So he blew very early.

But nobody was sleepy. They had had a good rest. They said, "Ho-hum, what a dark morning! I guess it's going to rain." The mothers made the fathers take their umbrellas to work, and that was all that happened.

"Pooh!" said Whistley Jim. "That wasn't much fun."

The next morning Whistley Jim still felt cranky. He said, "This time I won't blow until long after seven o'clock. Then they'll all be late. The boss will be very mad at the men. The teacher will scold the children. That will be fine! That will be fun!"

So he blew very late.

But all the people stretched and said, "Ho-hum, what a good long sleep!" The boss wasn't mad and the teacher didn't scold, because they were just as late as everybody else. And that was all that happened.

"Fiddlesticks!" said Whistley Jim. *"That wasn't much fun."*

The next morning Whistley Jim still felt cranky. He said, "Now I'll wait till the middle of the night, and I'll blow so hard I'll scare the wits out of everybody."

So he waited till all the fathers and mothers and children were asleep. Then he drew a deep breath. He blew the loudest he could blow. *"Toot, toot, toot! Toot, toot, toot! Toot, toot, toot!"* screamed Whistley Jim.

Now the fathers were also the firemen, in case of fire. Out of bed they jumped. "Fire!" they cried. They pulled on their trousers and shirts. They grabbed their firemen's hats. They rushed out of their houses and ran like everything to the firehouse.

Out came the fire engine, *clang, clang, clang!* The fathers jumped on. "Where's the fire?" cried the fathers. *Clang, clang, clang!* They rode all around Cloverdale, sniffing for smoke and making a great loud clang. Finally they said, "False alarm!" They drove the fire engine back.

Then the grocer, Mr. Henderson, invited all the fathers to his store. He unlocked the store. Even though it was the middle of the night, he got out some delicious cold ham and Swiss cheese. He fished big fat pickles out of a barrel. He passed around ham-and-cheese sandwiches and pickles. Mrs. Henderson got up and made a big pot of coffee in the kitchen back of the store.

"My, but that was fun—making a great loud *clang* and having sandwiches and coffee," said the fathers, as they took off their firemen's hats and went back to bed.

But Whistley Jim didn't enjoy it a bit. He was in a terrible temper. He wanted to do the worst thing he could possibly think of. Finally he said, "Tomorrow I won't blow at all! The people won't know when to get up or go to work or eat lunch or go home to supper. That will upset everybody, all right!"

So he didn't blow his time-to-get-up whistle. But not a father or a mother or a child was upset. Do you know what happened?

"This is a holiday!" said the fathers. "It's the Fourth of July! We won't go to work."

"We won't go to school!" said the children.

"We'll have chicken for dinner!" said the mothers.

They never gave a thought to Whistley Jim.

After dinner, the mothers and fathers and children put on their best clothes. They went for a walk. They listened to a band concert on the village green. When it got dark they had fireworks!

Red fireworks shot higher than Whistley Jim.

Whee-ee-ee! They whirled around in the sky.
Green fireworks shot even higher. Swish-sh-sh!
They showered Whistley Jim with sparks! *Bang!*
Bang, bang, bang! Fireworks that sounded like
big guns rocked Whistley Jim's factory with their
thunder.

Whistley Jim was scared out of his wits. But
nobody noticed. Everybody liked the fireworks
but Whistley Jim. My, but Whistley Jim was glad
when that holiday was over. He hadn't had a bit
of fun.

Early next morning the repair man came around, and very soon Whistley Jim felt fine and dandy again.

"I think I'll be good for a change," said Whistley Jim. He blew his time-to-get-up whistle right on the dot of seven. He didn't feel like being bad again for ages!

Mike the Taxi Man

Every morning at eight-thirty sharp, Mike the Taxi Man called at Tim Dexter's house to take Tim Dexter to school. Tim Dexter galloped down the walk, arms flying. He pointed his finger at Mike. He yelled, "B-b-b-b-b!" He leaped into the front seat.

Mike the Taxi Man and Tim Dexter called for Miranda Geneva. Miranda Geneva pranced down the walk, braids bobbing. She scrambled into the front seat.

Mike the Taxi Man and Tim Dexter and Miranda Geneva called for Susan Annabella. Susan Annabella skipped down the walk, curls dancing. She climbed into the front seat.

After that, they called for J. Edward, who bounced into one corner of the back, and Dorothy Lee, who wriggled into the other. They called for Carol Emmeline, who plunked herself in the middle. They called for Foster Douglas, Junior, who pushed in with both elbows. And finally they called for Jane, who climbed over lots of laps.

Mike the Taxi Man said, "All aboard! Next stop is the George Washington Thomas Jefferson Benjamin Franklin School!"

Whereupon everyone in the back seat stood up —because they just felt like standing up. They

wiggled. They leaned on the front seat. They
screeched in Mike the Taxi Man's ears. They
breathed in Mike the Taxi Man's neck.

They made Mike very nervous!

Mike was afraid they would bump their noses.
Mike stopped the car softly, putting out one hand
in front of Tim Dexter and Miranda Geneva and
Susan Annabella, so they wouldn't bump *their*
noses.

Mike pulled on the brake and sat back and

stared straight ahead and looked stern, and said in
a terrible voice, "J. Edward, Dorothy Lee, Carol
Emmeline, Foster Douglas, Junior, and Jane, stop
leaning on the front seat! Stop screeching in my
ears! Stop breathing in my neck! Stop wiggling
and *sit down!* Or we will not go one inch farther
toward the George Washington Thomas Jefferson
Benjamin Franklin School!"

So they sat down.

Next stop was the George Washington Thomas
Jefferson Benjamin Franklin School. Tim Dexter and Miranda Geneva and Susan Annabella
jumped out. They ran up the school walk. J. Edward and Dorothy Lee and Carol Emmeline and
Foster Douglas, Junior, got out and didn't even
shut the door. But Jane remembered to wave her
hand and say, "Good-by, Mike. See you later."

Mike the Taxi Man drove off.

At quarter of twelve Mike came back. He parked the car. He strolled up the walk with his hands in his pockets. He waited by the school door.

Out galloped Tim Dexter, arms flying. Out pranced Miranda Geneva, braids bobbing. Out skipped Susan Annabella, curls dancing. Out came J. Edward and Dorothy Lee and Carol Emmeline and Foster Douglas, Junior, and Jane.

But they didn't feel like riding in a taxi. They had been sitting down forever! Tim Dexter felt like yelling, "B-b-b-b-b!" Miranda Geneva felt like playing. Susan Annabella felt like hopping. J. Edward felt like scuffling. Dorothy Lee and Carol Emmeline felt like jumping. Foster Douglas, Junior, felt like screaming at the top of his lungs. And Jane felt like whirling around and around.

So that's what they did. They never even
looked at Mike.

Then Mike the Taxi Man took his hands out
of his pockets. He put his hands up to his mouth.
He took a deep breath and he shouted through
them like a horn, *"I'll bet nobody can beat me
to the car!"*

Tim Dexter stopped yelling. Miranda Geneva and Susan Annabella and J. Edward and Dorothy

Lee and Carol Emmeline and Foster Douglas, Junior, and Jane stopped playing and hopping and scuffling and jumping and screaming and

whirling around. They all looked at Mike. Mike the Taxi Man turned around and started for the car.

Tim Dexter began to run. Miranda Geneva and Susan Annabella flew after Tim. J. Edward and Dorothy Lee and Carol Emmeline and Foster Douglas, Junior, and Jane followed, fast as their legs would go.

They got to the car. Tim and Carol Emmeline pulled open the doors. They scrambled in in a heap, giggling and out of breath, before Mike even got there!

Mike said, "Shucks!"

Then Tim bounced into one corner of the back. Miranda Geneva wriggled into the other. Susan Annabella plunked herself right in the middle. J. Edward pushed in with both elbows. Dorothy Lee climbed over laps. Carol Emmeline and Foster Douglas, Junior, and Jane squeezed in front.

Mike started the car.

Whereupon everyone in the back seat stood up—because they just felt like standing up. They squirmed. They thumped on the front seat. They howled in Mike the Taxi Man's ears. They puffed in Mike the Taxi Man's neck. Tim Dexter yelled, "B-b-b-b-b!"

They made Mike very nervous!

Mike stopped the car softly, putting out his hand so the front-seat children wouldn't bump their noses.

Mike pulled on the brake and sat back and stared straight ahead and looked stern and said in a terrible voice, "Tim Dexter, Miranda Geneva, Susan Annabella, J. Edward, and Dorothy Lee, stop thumping on the front seat! Stop howling in my ears! Stop puffing in my neck! Stop yelling B-b-b-b-b! Stop squirming and *sit down!* Or we will spend the afternoon *right here!*"

So they sat down.

Then Mike took every child home to his own house. Up the walks they ran. But Jane remembered to wave her hand and say, "Good-by, Mike. See you tomorrow!"

The Cat That Wanted
To Be Useful

Skinny was a skinny black cat. He had a long, sad, bony face and a dirty, tangled coat. He was sad because he had no home. He was dirty because he was too sad to give himself a bath. His coat was tangled because he never took the trouble to get the tangles out.

Skinny knew many cats who were plump and handsome and had good homes. He knew an orange cat with a fluffy tail, a white cat with a pink nose, a maltese cat with beautiful whiskers, and a tiger cat with yellow eyes.

"They are beautiful," Skinny said to the wise old owl one night, "so they have good homes. I am skinny and homely. No one will give me a home."

"Rubbish," said the wise old owl. "Make your-

self useful," said the wise old owl, "and someone will give you a home."

"They will?" Skinny said. "Even if I'm homely, will they?" Skinny said.

"Sure they will," said the owl.

Skinny said, "How can I be useful?"

"That's for you to find out," said the owl.

Skinny started off to find out how he could be useful. Soon he saw something looming up in the dark. A big black dog stood at a gate. "Good evening," said Skinny. "Could I be useful to you in any way, and would you please give me a home?"

The big black dog said, "Yes, if you'll watch the house while I visit my friend the bulldog, and bark if anyone comes."

Skinny said, "I will gladly watch your house. I do want to be useful. But I don't know how to bark."

"Then you can't be useful to me," said the dog. Skinny went sadly along.

An old horse was standing in a field. "Good evening," said Skinny. "Could I be useful to you in any way, and would you please give me a home?"

The old horse said, "Yes, if you'll pull my wagon while I catch up on my rest."

Skinny said, "I would gladly pull your wagon. I do want to be useful. But I am too small and skinny to pull a wagon."

"Then you can't be useful to me," said the old horse. Skinny went sadly along.

Just after daylight he met a hen with her brood of chicks. He thought, My, she must be busy with so many children. Surely I can be useful here.

He said, "Good morning. Could I be useful to you in any way, and would you please give me a home?"

"You can *not* be useful to me," said the hen crossly. "I wouldn't trust you around my chicks for two minutes! Now be off!"

"Well, thank you," Skinny said. "Well, good-by."

It was morning. Skinny saw Mrs. Green sweeping her walk. He wanted to ask Mrs. Green whether he could be useful, but he was sure he could never sweep the walk or anything like that.

I'm no use to anybody! thought Skinny. He was so sad he crept under some bushes in Mrs. Green's yard and lay down. Skinny didn't know it, but the bushes were blueberry bushes. Blueberries were Mr. Green's favorite fruit. But he hardly ever got any berries from his bushes, because the minute a berry was ripe a blue jay darted down and ate it.

As Skinny lay under the bushes, a blue jay

darted down for a plump berry. He saw Skinny.
"Caw, caw!" shrieked the blue jay. Away he flew
without eating the berry.

When Mr. Green came home, Mrs. Green said,
"A cat is under our blueberry bushes. The blue
jays are afraid to come down. There are plenty of
blueberries for your supper."

Mr. Green said, "Fine!"

Mrs. Green said, "We must give that cat something to eat so he will stay and keep the blue jays away." She gave Skinny a dish of milk.

Skinny sat under the blueberry bushes. The berries grew big and ripe. Mr. Green had blueberries and cream. He had blueberry muffins. He had blueberry pie. He had blueberry waffles and blueberry cake and blueberry pancakes, too. He had never had so many delicious blueberries in his life, all because Skinny kept the blue jays away from the bushes.

Mrs. Green bought extra milk so Skinny could have plenty. Skinny could hardly believe his good

luck. He thought, Am I really being useful? Can it possibly be that I have a home?

He drank so much milk that he no longer looked skinny. He was so happy he gave himself a bath after every meal. He spent hours every day carefully smoothing his fur and biting the tangles out, till his coat shone like black silk.

At last the blueberry season was over. Mrs. Green picked the last berry. Suddenly Skinny knew that his job was done. Oh, thought Skinny, what will happen to me now? Mr. and Mrs. Green won't keep me when I am no longer useful.

But Mr. Green said, "That cat has done a good job. He has kept all the blue jays away."

Mrs. Green said, "And he didn't hurt a single bird, either."

Mr. Green said, "We can't turn out a cat that has done such a good job for us."

Mrs. Green said, "Of course not. Let's keep him. He can be our cat." Then Mrs. Green looked at Skinny, and she said to Mr. Green, "Do you know what? Now that he isn't skinny and his coat is smooth and he doesn't look so sad, he's really a very handsome cat!"

And when Skinny heard that—well, how would *you* feel, if you were Skinny?

Where Is the Carrousel?

Ricky and his mother were on their way to the zoo.

His mother said, "Here is some money for crackerjack to feed the elephants. We'll see all the animals. Then we'll find the carrousel."

Ricky said, "What kind of animal is *that?*"

His mother said, "You'll be surprised!"

Ricky bought some crackerjack. He and his

mother came to an animal's yard with a great big fence around it. A great big animal was sloshing around in a pool.

Ricky said, "Is that a carrousel?"

His mother said, "Hippopotamus."

Ricky went on. He saw a big animal with a long trunk. He said, "I know *that's* not a carrousel. Because *that's* an elephant." He threw some crisp, crunchy crackerjack for the elephant to pick up with his trunk. He said, "I'll save some crackerjack to feed the carrousel." Ricky's mother smiled.

Ricky went into the monkey house. He saw little monkeys, big monkeys, middle-sized monkeys. They were swinging on their bars. They were playing with their brothers. They were looking at the people who were looking at them. But Ricky didn't see a carrousel.

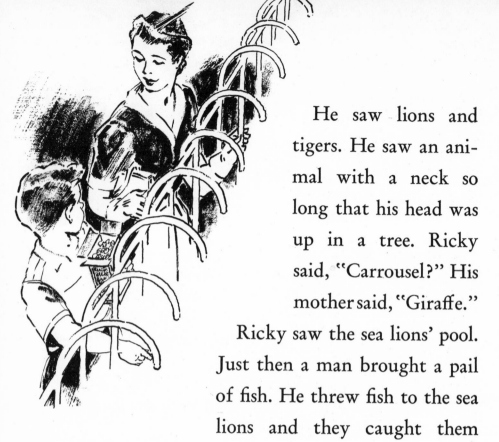

He saw lions and tigers. He saw an animal with a neck so long that his head was up in a tree. Ricky said, "Carrousel?" His mother said, "Giraffe."

Ricky saw the sea lions' pool. Just then a man brought a pail of fish. He threw fish to the sea lions and they caught them smack in their mouths. When Ricky saw the fish he said, "I'm hungry."

His mother said, "We'll have some lunch. Then we'll find the carrousel."

Ricky had a peanut butter sandwich, a glass of milk, and a dish of vanilla ice cream. He ate at a table that had an umbrella to keep the sun away.

He said, "Now let's find the carrousel." So they started to find it.

Ricky's mother asked a man cleaning up papers, "Which way is the carrousel?"

The man said, "Turn right. Up the steps by the polar bears' cave."

They turned right, up the steps by the polar bears' cave. Ricky said, "We're going *away* from the zoo!"

His mother said, "That sign says *To the Car-*

rousel." They went along a path toward the carrousel.

Ricky said, "I'll give the carrousel the rest of my crackerjack." His mother laughed. Ricky said, "What's so funny?"

His mother said, "You'll find out." His mother said to a man cutting grass, "Which way is the carrousel?"

The man said, "Straight ahead through the tunnel."

Ricky pulled his mother through the tunnel. When they came out of the tunnel, his mother said, "Do you hear anything?"

Ricky said, "I hear some music."

They went a little farther. His mother said, "Do you see anything?"

Ricky said, "I think I see—a MERRY-GO-ROUND!"

His mother said, "Well, that's the carrousel!"

Ricky looked very surprised. Then Ricky looked at his mother. He and his mother laughed and laughed because Ricky had said, "I'll give the carrousel my crackerjack!"

After that Ricky had four rides on a horse that went up and down. Every time he passed his mother, she waved the crackerjack box. And they both laughed some more!

Butch the Bulldozer

*C*lank, *rumble, clank,* came Butch the Bulldozer. He was coming to dig up the ground
so some houses could be built. He was feeling big.
He was feeling strong. He felt like bulldozing
today.

There was a row of houses facing one way.
There was a row facing the other way. Between
their backyards was a patch of woods. Butch the

Bulldozer was going to cut down the woods. He was going to dig up the ground.

Clank, rumble, clank, he came up to the woods. Then he stopped.

It was a pretty patch of woods. Tall trees waved their branches in the spring breeze. Bushes and flowers blossomed. A little brook gurgled along. Butch listened to the leaves rustling. He listened to the birds singing. He listened to the brook bubbling. Still, Butch felt like bulldozing. He was going to cut down the flowers and rustling trees. He was going to fill up the bubbling brook.

Three little heads popped out of the green leaves on a tall tree. Six little eyes looked at Butch the Bulldozer. "*Squawk, squawk, squawk!*" screamed three baby birds.

The mother bird came flying to the tall tree. She perched on her nest. She looked down at Butch. "What are you doing here?" said the mother bird.

"I'm going to bulldoze this woods," said Butch the Bulldozer.

"Why?" said the mother bird.

"To build houses," said Butch.

"Don't be silly," said the mother bird. "We have enough houses here now."

Butch looked around. "No houses at all," said Butch the Bulldozer rudely.

"What do you call *this?*" cried the mother bird. She fluttered off the nest so Butch could see. Butch

saw the round nest hidden in the leaves. The
mother bird had carefully woven it of twigs and
grass. She had shaped it to hold the speckled eggs.
She had lined it with soft feathers and bits of
cloth. "Could anyone ask for a better house?" said
the mother bird proudly.

Just then three little heads popped out of a hole
in the tree trunk. Six little eyes peered at Butch.
"Chitter, chitter!" chattered three baby squirrels.

The mother squirrel came scurrying through

the bushes. She ran up the tree and sat on a limb. She looked at Butch. "What are you doing here?" she said.

"I'm going to bulldoze this woods," said Butch the Bulldozer.

"Why?" said the mother squirrel.

"To build houses," said Butch.

"Don't be silly," said the mother squirrel. "We have plenty of houses here now."

Butch looked around.

"What do you call *this?*" cried the mother squirrel. She jerked her tail toward the hole in the old tree trunk.

Butch saw the hole in the tree where the baby squirrels lived. The mother squirrel had hunted till she found a high, safe hole. The hole was deep and warm. She had lined it with scraps of paper and bits of her own fur.

"Could anyone ask for a better house?" said the mother squirrel proudly.

A baby rabbit hopped in front of Butch and wiggled his nose in alarm. The mother rabbit came hopping through the cool green grass. "What are you doing here?" said the mother rabbit.

"I'm going to bulldoze this woods," said Butch the Bulldozer. "At least, I think I'm going to."

"Why?" said the mother rabbit.

"To build houses, of course!" said Butch crossly.

"Don't be silly," said the mother rabbit. "We have all kinds of houses."

Butch looked around.

"See this!" cried the mother rabbit. She hopped to one side so Butch could see her home. Butch saw a little hole in the ground. The mother rabbit had dug this hole for her babies' secret house. The hole was hidden under grass and roots and leaves, so no one else would know where the baby rabbits lived.

"Could anyone ask for a better house?" said the mother rabbit proudly.

A tiny frog came leaping out of the brook. When he saw Butch the Bulldozer, he gave a baby croak. The mother frog leaped up beside him and looked at Butch. "What are you doing here?" said the mother frog. "I'm going to bulldoze this woods!" said Butch. "I mean I *was* going to," he added.

"Why?" said the mother frog.

"Oh, for goodness' sake!" said Butch. "To build houses, of course."

"Don't be ridiculous," said the mother frog. "*This* is better than any house." The mother frog

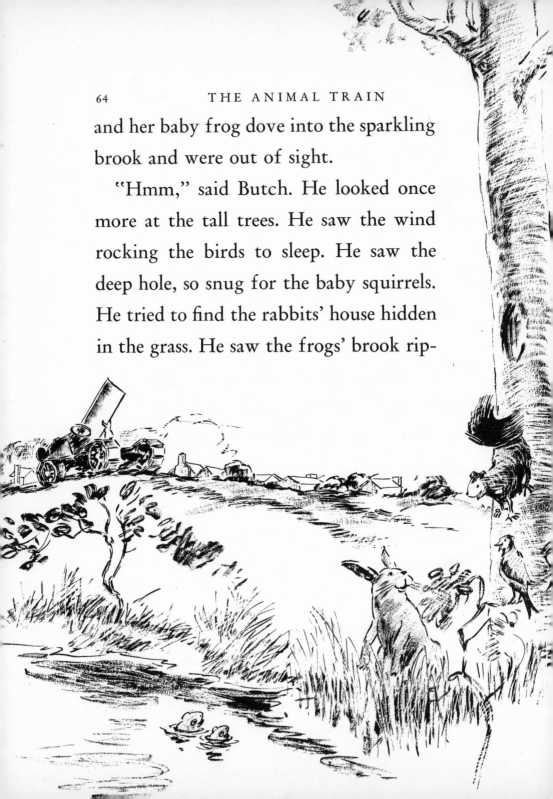

and her baby frog dove into the sparkling
brook and were out of sight.

"Hmm," said Butch. He looked once
more at the tall trees. He saw the wind
rocking the birds to sleep. He saw the
deep hole, so snug for the baby squirrels.
He tried to find the rabbits' house hidden
in the grass. He saw the frogs' brook rip-

pling happily by. "Excuse me, I made a mistake," said Butch. "I'll find another place to bulldoze."

Clank, rumble, clank. Butch the Bulldozer backed away. He turned around. He went clumping down the street. The birds and squirrels and rabbits and frogs sang and chattered and wiggled and croaked for joy.

And out of the houses in this row, and out of the houses in that row, came the boys and girls. They ran into the woods. They smelled the flowers. They played among the trees. They waded in the brook. The boys and girls had a picnic by the brook. And they tossed their crumbs to the birds and squirrels and rabbits and even the frogs, so *they* had a picnic too!

Johnnycake for Ronnie

One thing about Ronnie, he was always forgetting. He forgot the bunch of marigolds he meant to take to his teacher. He forgot to bring his mittens home from school. He forgot where he left his little red fire engine.

Ronnie's grandma said, "Ronnie, you would forget your head if it wasn't fastened on!"

"Betcha I wouldn't," said Ronnie.

"Betcha you would," said Grandma.

Another thing about Ronnie, he liked good things to eat. He liked fried chicken. He liked mashed potatoes and gravy. He liked chocolate cake and coconut custard pie and gingerbread with whipped cream. But what he liked to eat best of all was the old-fashioned johnnycake that Grandma made when she came to visit. This old-fashioned johnnycake was yellow. It was crunchy and crisp. Ronnie ate it warm, with butter melting on it.

One day Ronnie's grandma was visiting him. Ronnie was galloping around the yard on his pretend horse, yelling, "Yippee!"

"Ronnie, please go to the store," Ronnie's grandma called. "Buy a package of yellow corn meal and I will make some johnnycake for supper."

Ronnie said, "Yippee!"

His grandma said, "Can you remember that?"

Ronnie said, "Sure!" He took the money. He galloped toward the store on his pretend horse. He met his friend Billy and stopped to play cowboy.

Pretty soon Ronnie said, "I forgot! I've got to go to the store." He galloped on toward the store. Then he met his friend Henry and stopped to play cowboy with him.

After a while Ronnie said, "I forgot! I've got to go to the store." When he reached the store he hitched his pretend horse and went inside. Then he thought, What did Grandma tell me to buy?

The store man said, "What can I do for you this morning?"

Ronnie thought and thought. He said, "I know. Some kind of cake."

"How about a coconut cake?" said the store man.

Ronnie shook his head.

"Fruitcake?" said the man.

"No," said Ronnie.

"Chocolate cake? Poundcake? Cupcakes?" said the man.

"They look good. But they don't sound right," said Ronnie.

"Look around," said the man. "You'll remember."

Ronnie looked at cakes and cookies. He looked at cheese crackers and pretzels. "Wish I had a pretzel," said Ronnie. Then he said, "Oh, I forgot. I was trying to remember."

He moved to another shelf. This shelf had perfectly delicious things. There were dill pickles. There were mixed-up pickles. There were fat green olives with red in the middle. "I could eat a dill pickle," said Ronnie, his mouth watering. Then he said, "Oh, I forgot. I *must* remember that thing I'm supposed to get!"

He moved to another shelf. Now he was looking at things in cans. There were canned peas, which he liked, and succotash, which he liked. "Yum! Ravioli!" said Ronnie.

There were cans of pineapple and cans of figs and cans of fruit cocktail with cherries in it. "What *was* I supposed to get?" said Ronnie.

"Have you remembered yet?" said the store man, coming around.

"Not yet," said Ronnie.

"Maybe it wasn't a cake," said the man. "Maybe she said a cake of chocolate. Did she say a cake of chocolate?"

"No," said Ronnie.

"Did she say a cake of soap?" said the man.

"Nah!" said Ronnie. He moved to the meat counter. There were chickens and lamb chops and pork chops and steaks, which Ronnie liked. There was chopped meat, which he liked even more. There were frankfurters, which he liked most of all.

"Oh, boy, I'm hungry!" said Ronnie.

"Maybe your grandmother said chopped meat to make meat cakes," the store man said.

"No," said Ronnie.

The store man began to clean up the store. Finally he was ready to close. "Say, Johnny," said the store man. He called Ronnie Johnny because he didn't know his name. "You better go home and . . ."

"Johnnycake!" shouted Ronnie.

"Huh?" said the store man.

"That's what my grandmother said!" Ronnie cried.

"We don't have any," said the store man.

"She's going to make some," Ronnie explained. "I'm supposed to get . . ." He looked around at all the shelves. "What do you put in johnny-cake?" he said.

"Flour?" asked the store man.

"No," said Ronnie.

"Butter, eggs?" asked the man.

"No," said Ronnie.

"What is this johnnycake?" the store man asked.

"It's sort of flat," said Ronnie. "It's crisp and crunchy. It's all yellow."

"Yellow?" said the man. "Corn meal?" asked the man.

"Yellow corn meal!" Ronnie shouted. "That's what she said!"

The man put the box of corn meal in a bag. Ronnie felt in his jacket pockets. He felt in his pants pockets. He said, "I forget where I put the money." He felt in his blouse pocket. "Here it is!" He started out the door.

"You forgot the corn meal," called the man.

Ronnie came back and got the package of corn meal.

"You forgot the change," said the man. Ronnie came back and got the change. He started home. "Oh, I forgot my horse!" said Ronnie. He went back and unhitched his pretend horse.

Ronnie galloped home. His grandma said, "My

goodness gracious, I thought you'd forgotten to come home. Did you remember to bring me the corn meal?"

Ronnie said, "Grandma, did you think I'd forget an easy thing like *that? Here* is your yellow corn meal!"

Mrs. Hen's Vacation

Mrs. Hen got up with the sun. She woke the chicks. She scurried to get breakfast. She shooed the chicks out to play. She called out to the chicks, "Whatever you're doing, stop it this minute!"

Then she swept up the crumbs. She washed the clothes. She went to market. She baked cookies. She sewed on buttons.

Finally she called, "Here, chick, chick, chick!" She tucked the chicks into bed. She brought them a drink. She picked up their toys.

She sat down and sighed. "No one ever worked so hard!" Mrs. Hen said. "I need a vacation from all my hard work."

Next morning she said to the baby chicks, "This is my vacation. You must get your own breakfast. I shall stay in bed."

The baby chicks tiptoed out, looking very surprised.

Then Mrs. Hen thought, I wonder if those baby chicks will eat their cereal. She got up to see that the baby chicks ate their cereal.

Mrs. Hen looked around her house. She said, "While I am on vacation I shall get a maid to sweep up the crumbs." She got a maid to sweep up the crumbs.

She said, "I shall send all the clothes out to the laundry." She sent all the clothes out to the laundry.

She said, "I shall buy some cookies instead of baking." She bought some cookies.

Mrs. Hen said, "I will not sew on one single

button!" She gave the baby chicks some pins to hold up their dungarees.

Then Mrs. Hen said, "I need a better vacation. I shall get a baby sitter to stay with my chicks while I go and visit my friends." She got a baby sitter. She packed her suitcase. She put on her hat with blue cornflowers on it and went to visit her friends.

The first friend Mrs. Hen visited said, "Sit down and wait for me while I sweep up these crumbs."

Mrs. Hen said, "Oh, no! I am on my vacation from sweeping crumbs." She thought to herself. I wonder if that baby sitter swept up the crumbs neatly.

The second friend Mrs. Hen visited said, "I am just going out to market. Won't you come along with me?"

Mrs. Hen said, "Oh, no! I am on my vacation from markets." She thought to herself, I wonder if that baby sitter remembered to buy the right cereal.

The third friend Mrs. Hen visited said, "You may help me put my babies to bed."

Mrs. Hen said, "Oh, no indeed! I am on my vacation from putting babies to bed!" She thought to herself, I wonder if that baby sitter tucked the covers in.

Mrs. Hen went along, looking at the scenery. She thought, I'm having a good vacation. It certainly is wonderful not to sweep up crumbs. Then she thought, I wish I could tuck my baby chicks into bed.

Mrs. Hen went along, smelling the flowers. She thought, I'm having a fine vacation! It certainly is wonderful not to go to market. Then she thought, I wish I could kiss my baby chicks good night.

Mrs. Hen went along, enjoying the evening breeze. She thought, I'm having a wonderful vacation! With that, big tears rolled down Mrs. Hen's cheeks. "Oh," cried Mrs. Hen, "how I miss my baby chicks! I am going back home this very minute!"

Mrs. Hen turned around and flapped her wings and flew and scurried toward home as fast as she could go. She was so glad to see her baby chicks again that she woke them up to kiss them all good night.

Next morning Mrs. Hen got up with the sun. She woke the chicks. She scurried around getting breakfast.

She called, "Whatever you're doing, stop it this minute!"

She washed the clothes, clucking happily to herself. She took all the chicks to market and let the littlest one ride with the groceries. She baked a big batch of chocolate cookies and let the chicks lick the bowl. She gave the chicks an extra helping of cereal for supper. She tucked them all into bed and took each one of them a drink of water.

Then Mrs. Hen sat down, humming to herself, and began to sew on buttons. "My," Mrs. Hen said to herself, "that was a fine vacation, all right. But my!" said Mrs. Hen. "I'm certainly glad it's over!"

The Shiny Red Rubber Boots

Every morning when Bobby got up, his mother said, "Get dressed, dear. Put on your shoes. Tie your shoelaces."

Every morning Bobby said, "Where *are* my shoes?"

Every morning Mother said, "Where did you leave them?"

Bobby said, "I don't remember."

Mother said, "You never remember."

"Oh, here's one shoe down in this chair!" Bobby said.

"Did you drop the other in the hall?" said Mother. "What's that bump under the rug? Well! How in the world could your shoe get here in the wastebasket!"

"When will you *ever*," said Mother, with a great big sigh, "put your shoes in the closet or neatly under the bed!"

On Bobby's birthday Bobby got a pair of boots —shiny red rubber boots. Mother said to him, "We'll put these boots in your closet until you need them."

The next morning when Bobby got out of bed, his mother said, "Get dressed, dear. Put on your shoes."

Bobby found one shoe in his toy truck, the

other under his pillow. He was just going to put them on when he remembered his boots, his shiny red rubber boots. So he put his shoes under the bed, neatly side by side. He put his boots on. He went clump, clumping to breakfast.

Daddy said, "Good morning, Butch. And why have you got your boots on this fine day?"

Bobby looked down at his shiny red boots. They twinkled at him. He couldn't quite think why he had them on, but he knew there was some good reason. He said, "Because." He wiggled his

boots to make them twinkle while he was eating his breakfast.

After breakfast Bobby went clump, clumping out to play. He saw Emily. She said, "Bobby, it isn't cold. Why have you got your boots on?"

Bobby watched his boots twinkle. He said, "Because."

Then he rode his bike. He met Mrs. Stuart. She

said, "Bobby, it isn't raining. Why have you got your boots on?"

Bobby said, "Because."

He met the mailman. The mailman said, "Bobby, it isn't muddy today. Why have you got your boots on?"

Bobby said, "Because."

He rode his bike home, watching his boots twinkle. Mother said, "Come on, we're going to the store."

The man in the store saw Bobby. He saw the red rubber boots. He said, "Hello, boots! Where are you going with that cowboy?"

Bobby looked at the man and looked at his boots and looked at the man again. Now he knew the reason! He said to Mother on the way home, "Know why I'm wearing my new red boots?"

"No. Why?" said Mother.

"Because I'm a cowboy," Bobby said.

When he got home he went clump, clumping to Emily's house. He said, "Know why I'm wearing my new red boots?"

"No. Why?" said Emily.

"Because I'm a cowboy," Bobby said.

He went clump, clumping to Mrs. Stuart's. He said, "Know why I'm wearing my new red boots?"

"No. Why?" said Mrs. Stuart.

"Because I'm a cowboy," Bobby said.

He went clump, clumping toward home and met the mailman again. He said, "Know why I'm wearing my new red boots?"

"Why are you?" said the mailman.

"Because I'm a cowboy, of course," Bobby said. He went clump, clumping home.

Mother said, "Come on, we're going to take

our nap now." They went into Bobby's bedroom.

Bobby said, "Do cowboys take naps?"

Mother said, "They certainly *do!*"

Bobby got undressed, all but his boots. He said, "Do cowboys wear their boots to bed when they take their naps?"

Mother said, "They certainly *don't!* They put their boots under the bed, neatly side by side, so they can find them quickly when the head cowboy calls them."

Bobby said, "Oh." He took off his boots. He

saw his shoes under the bed where he had put them that morning. He said, "I'll put my shoes in the closet in case I need them again." He put his boots under the bed very, very neatly.

"That's the way cowboys *always* do," said Bobby, as he bounced into bed.

A Sandwich for Smoky

Smoky was a good old horse. His job was pulling a wagon. The wagon was loaded with junk. *Clop, clop,* went Smoky, pulling his load. *Clink, clink,* went the bells on the junk wagon.

When they heard *clink, clink, clop, clop,* the children came running—especially Agatha, Alan, and Archie. They patted Smoky. They gave him sugar. Smoky munched the sugar. Mmm! It was delicious.

That was on Monday, Tuesday, Wednesday. That was on Thursday, Friday, Saturday. Sunday was Smoky's day off.

On Sunday Smoky was free to wander along the bank of the river without his harness and eat the green grass. Oh, it felt wonderful with no harness, no load to pull. Smoky tossed his head. He sniffed the air. He nibbled the green grass. He looked around at all the people having picnics.

One Sunday when Smoky was wandering along the bank of the river nibbling the green grass, he found something in the grass. Smoky said, "What's this?" Smoky turned the thing over with his nose.

Smoky took a nibble. "Mmm!" said Smoky. It was a ham sandwich someone had dropped. Smoky ate the sandwich. He munched and munched and smacked his lips. He had never tasted a sandwich before. It was delicious! He looked around hungrily for more sandwiches.

All the next week while he was pulling the junk wagon–*clop, clop*–Smoky thought about the sandwich. He thought about it Monday, Tuesday, Wednesday. He thought about it Thursday, Friday, Saturday. He thought about it when Agatha, Alan, and Archie patted him and gave him sugar. The sugar was good, but it wasn't as good as that sandwich.

Next Sunday Smoky was free again to wander along the bank of the river. Again he tossed his head and sniffed the air. Then he looked around for a sandwich. He couldn't find one in the grass. But he saw a lady eating. He headed straight for her.

The lady said, "Get away!" The lady said,

"Help!" She put her coat over her sandwiches so Smoky wouldn't get them. She scrambled away quickly.

Smoky nosed the coat. He could smell the sandwiches. He gave a good yank with his teeth. *R-r-i-p!* went the coat. There were the sandwiches underneath.

Smoky ate the sandwiches. Mmm! They were

chicken. He munched and munched and smacked his lips. Those sandwiches were delicious! He looked around for more sandwiches.

All the next week while he was pulling the junk wagon—*clop, clop*—Smoky thought about the sandwiches. He thought about them when Agatha, Alan, and Archie patted him and gave him sugar. The sugar was good, but it wasn't as good as those sandwiches.

Next Sunday, when Smoky was free to wander along the bank of the river, he looked right away for more sandwiches. He couldn't find one in the grass. He didn't see a lady eating. Then he saw a fisherman, fishing in the river and chewing on a great thick sandwich. Smoky headed straight for him.

The fisherman said, "Get out!"

Smoky stretched out his neck to get the sandwich. Smoky opened his mouth, he was so hungry for that sandwich.

The fisherman yelled, "Police!" The fisherman leaned over backward to get away from Smoky. *Splash*, he fell into the river.

Smoky snatched the sandwich just in time. He ate the sandwich. Mmm! It was boloney. Smoky munched and munched and smacked his lips. That sandwich was delicious.

He was about to look around for more sandwiches when suddenly, right beside him, stood the fisherman, dripping wet. And right beside the fisherman stood a policeman!

"So you're the one that's making the trouble!" the policeman said. "If I hadn't seen it with my own two eyes, I'd never believe it. Come along to the judge."

Sadly, head down, Smoky came, *clop, clop*.

The lady whose coat he had torn came along, carrying her coat. The fisherman came too, dripping wet and carrying his fishing rod.

The judge said, "A good, dependable horse like you, stealing sandwiches!"

The lady said, "Ruining coats!"

The fisherman said, "Pushing folks in the river!"

The judge said, "Oh, my!" and shook his head. He said to Smoky, "I fine you a hundred dollars."

At that moment the children arrived. Agatha, Alan, and Archie got there just as the judge was speaking.

"Fifty for me for ruining my coat," said the lady loudly.

"Fifty for me for pushing me in," said the fisherman, very mad.

Smoky hung his head. He didn't have a hundred dollars. "Then off you go to jail," said the judge.

The children looked at each other. Agatha said, "I have a penny. Smoky can have that to pay his fine."

The lady said, "Fifty dollars!"

The fisherman said, "Fifty!"

Alan said, "I have a knife. Smoky can have that to pay his fine."

"Well, ten dollars," said the lady.

"Not a cent less," said the fisherman.

Archie said, "I have a top. Smoky can have that to pay his fine."

"Oh, well," said the lady, "I was tired of this coat anyway."

"Oh, well," said the fisherman, "it was nice and cool in the river."

Off went the lady to buy a more stylish coat. Off went the fisherman to buy another boloney sandwich before he went back to fishing.

The judge said to the children, "Well, how are you going to keep this horse from eating sandwiches? How are you going to keep this horse from pushing folks in the river?"

Agatha, Alan, and Archie thought.

Agatha said, "We'll bring him a picnic lunch every week."

Alan said, "With sandwiches in it."

Archie said, "Then he won't eat other people's lunch."

The judge said, "O.K."

So every Sunday, on his day off, Smoky was free to wander along the bank of the river. Oh, it felt wonderful with no harness, no load to pull! And every Sunday Agatha, Alan, and Archie brought him a nice lunch, with ham, chicken, and boloney sandwiches wrapped in wax paper—and pickles, too.

Dawdling Douglas

D ouglas was a boy who dawdled. That means
he took his own sweet time. He dawdled
over getting dressed. He dawdled over breakfast.
He dawdled over going to school until he was
always late.

Douglas's mother said, "Douglas, don't dawdle. Get dressed. Eat your breakfast. Go right
along to school."

Douglas said, "You *never* let me have fun!"

His mother said, "Some day I'm going to let you dawdle till you're good and tired of dawdling."

Douglas said, "Can I dawdle till I'm good and tired tomorrow?"

So next day Mother didn't say, "Douglas, don't dawdle."

He dawdled about getting up. When he came downstairs, his brother Bill and his sister Polly and his little sister Roseanne were eating. Douglas said, "What? Soup for breakfast?"

"Soup for lunch," said Mother. "This is lunchtime for folks who don't dawdle. But you may have breakfast."

Douglas didn't mind. "You said I could dawdle," he said.

"Go ahead and dawdle," said Mother.

Douglas dawdled over breakfast. He went out to play. He played and dawdled. Finally he went to school. The children were just going home. "Fine time to get here," said Douglas's teacher. "Sit down and do some arithmetic."

Douglas dawdled so over his arithmetic that when he went home it was almost dark. Mother was putting dinner on the table.

Douglas cried, "Mmm! Beefsteak!"

"Beefsteak for us," said Mother. "This is our dinner. But soup for you. This is your lunch." Douglas ate spinach soup.

Mother said, "By the way, are you tired of dawdling yet?"

Douglas didn't care quite so much about dawdling now. But he said, "Oh, no!"

Mother said, "You may go out and play."

Douglas said, "It's dark!"

"You always go out to play after your lunch," said Mother.

Douglas didn't want her to know he was tired of dawdling. He went out. It was cold and dark. He certainly didn't feel like dawdling out here. He went in.

Mother said, "Good night, dear."

Douglas said, "May I have something to eat before I go to bed?"

"Oh, you're not going to bed," said Mother. "You just had your lunch. We're going to bed, but you may play and dawdle as long as you like."

Douglas watched Mother, Daddy, Bill, Polly, and Roseanne go upstairs. He thought how good his bed would feel. He thought he might tiptoe up. But he wouldn't admit he was tired of dawdling. So he didn't go.

It was very still. Douglas heard the house creak. He thought he heard a footstep. His hair stood up on end.

Dawdling was the last thing on earth he wanted to do! But he wouldn't give in and go to bed. He curled up in a chair and shut his eyes tight.

Next thing he knew, Mother was saying, "Well, dear, did you have fun, dawdling all night?"

Douglas opened his eyes and blinked at the

sun. He said, "Sure!" Goodness, was he glad that night was over! He was so hungry he could eat a house.

No one else was up. "Let's see," Mother said. "You had lunch last night. Now I shall get your dinner."

"Beefsteak?" said Douglas hungrily.

Mother said, "I'm sorry. Bill and Polly and Roseanne ate up the steak. You will have to have eggs for your dinner." Douglas sat down to his dinner. Mother sat down to her breakfast. "It must be fun, dawdling as long as you want to," Mother said. "After you eat your dinner you may play and dawdle some more. When you're good and ready, you may go to bed."

Douglas didn't want to go to bed this lovely morning. But he didn't want to tell Mother he was tired of dawdling. He finished his cereal. He ate two scrambled eggs. He drank two glasses of milk. He ate three pieces of toast. He ate six strips of bacon.

He said, "I was just thinking. Could I pretend this is breakfast?"

Mother said, "I suppose you could."

Douglas said, "O.K." He felt much more cheerful. He ate another scrambled egg and another piece of toast, with currant jelly on it. He thought of something surprising and very pleasant. "Hey," said Douglas in amazed delight, "I'm up early this morning!"

"Why, so you are!" said Mother.

Just then they heard a thump upstairs as if someone was getting up. "What are those kids dawdling for?" said Douglas in disgust. "Why don't those kids get up? They're going to be late to school if they don't look out."

"But *you* won't be late," said Mother. "You're up so early. Isn't it nice to have an early start!"

"You bet!" said Douglas.

What the Mother Animals Whispered

Janie had a new doll. It had curly brown hair and blue eyes that opened and closed and real eyelashes.

"What shall I name my new dolly?" Janie wondered.

She thought of the names of some children she liked. There was Judy in school. "I might name her Judy," Janie said.

There were Carolyn and Nancy and Dorothy and Shirley in Sunday school. "Those are nice names," Janie said.

There were Karen and Ann in dancing school. "Karen and Ann are awfully pretty names," Janie said.

But she couldn't decide whether to name her doll Judy or Carolyn or Nancy or Dorothy or Shirley or Karen or Ann. Janie took her dolly and went outdoors. She walked up and down, thinking.

A gray squirrel came scurrying down a tree and stood upside down on the trunk, looking at Janie. That's the mother squirrel to the baby squirrels, Janie thought. She must be hungry. Janie ran indoors to find a nut for the squirrel. She threw it on the ground. The mother squirrel looked at the nut, then ran and picked it up. She held the nut in her front paws and cracked it with her teeth.

I think I'll ask the squirrel what to name my new dolly, Janie thought. She held up her doll so the squirrel could see, and asked her what to name it.

"I always name my babies Bushy Tail," said the squirrel, munching the nut.

"But my dolly hasn't got a bushy tail!" Janie said.

"She hasn't?" said the squirrel in surprise, dropping a piece of shell. "Well, it doesn't matter what you name her," said the squirrel. "I never call my babies by their real name, anyway. I just call them . . ." The squirrel stopped talking to finish her nut. She dropped the last of the shell on the ground and turned to scamper away. As she went, she whispered something to Janie. Then

she whisked up the tree to her baby squirrels.

Janie ran into the house. "Know what the mother squirrel calls her babies?" Janie cried to Mother. She whispered in Mother's ear what the squirrel had whispered to her.

"She *does?*" said Mother.

Janie went out again with her doll. The squirrel was nowhere to be seen. But there on the front lawn hopped a plump, bright-eyed robin. That's the mother robin to the baby robins, Janie thought. I'll ask the mother robin what I should name my dolly.

She held up her doll so the robin could see, and asked her what to name it.

"I name all my babies Red Breast," the mother robin told her.

"That would be a funny name for a dolly!" Janie said, laughing.

"It would?" said the mother robin. "Well, it doesn't matter, anyway. I just call them . . ." Just then a tiny tinkle of a bell startled the robin. She stopped talking and flew away. As she soared over Janie's head, she whispered something to her.

Janie ran into the house. "Know what the mother robin calls her babies?" Janie cried to Mother. She whispered in Mother's ear what the robin had whispered to her.

"She *does?*" said Mother.

Janie went out again with her doll. The robin was nowhere to be seen. But the pussy whose bell had startled the robin was sitting there in the sunshine. That's the mother kitty to the baby kitties next door, Janie thought. I'll ask the mother kitty what I should name my dolly.

She held up her doll so the kitty could see, and asked her what to name it.

"I have a rule for naming my babies," said the mother cat. "If they're black, I call them Blackie. If they're tiger cats, I call them Tiger. That's simple enough."

"But my dolly isn't black and she isn't a tiger, either," Janie explained.

"Oh, well," said the mother cat. "Names aren't important. I never call my babies by their real names, anyway."

"What do you call them?" Janie asked.

"I call them . . ." Just then a dog came around the house. The mother cat stopped talking. She yawned and stretched to show the dog she wasn't afraid. Then she walked away to make sure her babies were safe. As she walked away, she said something softly to Janie.

Janie ran into the house. "Know what the mother kitty calls her babies?" Janie cried to Mother. She whispered in Mother's ear what the kitty had whispered to her.

"Does she *really?*" said Mother.

Janie went out again with her doll. The kitty was nowhere to be seen, but the dog was there and happy to see Janie. Janie sat down on the step. That's the mother doggie to the baby doggies who live down the street, Janie thought. I'll ask the mother doggie what I should name my dolly.

She held up her doll so the doggie could see, and asked her what to name it.

The mother dog sniffed the doll all over. She

gave Janie's hand a kiss with her soft tongue. She looked up at Janie with kind brown eyes. "I mostly name my babies Cuddles," said the mother dog, "though sometimes I name them Snooks. How do you like those?"

"I don't like them," said Janie.

"Neither do I," said the mother dog. "Well, one time I had a baby with a beautiful name. Her name was Leontine Lucile Marie Josephine Victoria Louise. Do you like that name?"

"Yes!" said Janie. "But it's awfully long."

"I thought so too," said the mother dog. "So I called Leontine Lucile Marie Josephine Victoria Louise just what I call all the others."

"What?" asked Janie.

The dog heard someone calling. She pricked up her ears. She got up and hurried off to look after her babies. As she went, she whispered something quickly in Janie's ear.

Janie sat on the step for a few minutes, holding her doll. She was thinking. She got up and went in to Mother. "Now I know what name to give my dolly!" she said. "I'm going to name her Judy Carolyn Nancy Dorothy Shirley Karen Ann!"

"Why, that's a beautiful name!" said Mother. "But isn't it very long?"

"That doesn't matter," said Janie. "I won't call her that."

"What will you call her?" asked Mother, smiling at Janie.

Janie thought of what the squirrel mother had told her, what the bright-eyed robin had whispered in her ear, what the mother kitty and the brown-eyed doggie had said.

"I'm just going to call her Honey!" said Janie.